Mrs. Sewell

The Children of Summerbrook

Anatiposi

Mrs. Sewell

The Children of Summerbrook

Reprint of the original, first published in 1859.

1st Edition 2023 | ISBN: 978-3-38230-667-0

Anatiposi Verlag is an imprint of Outlook Verlagsgesellschaft mbH.

Verlag (Publisher): Outlook Verlag GmbH, Zeilweg 44, 60439 Frankfurt, Deutschland
Vertretungsberechtigt (Authorized to represent): E. Roepke, Zeilweg 44, 60439 Frankfurt, Deutschland
Druck (Print): Books on Demand GmbH, In de Tarpen 42, 22848 Norderstedt, Deutschland

THE CHILDREN OF SUMMERBROOK:

SCENES OF VILLAGE LIFE,

DESCRIBED IN SIMPLE VERSE.

BY MRS. SEWELL,

Author of "Homely Ballads."

LONDON: JARROLD AND SONS,
47, ST. PAUL'S CHURCHYARD.

CONTENTS.

	PAGE
SUMMERBROOK	3
JENNY LEE	5
THE SHEPHERD'S CHILD	7
THE LAZY GIRL	9
THE DIRTY LANE	11
NELLY WHITE	14
DANIEL DAY	17
THE HAPPY HOME	18
LITTLE PATTY	22
THE CROSS GIRLS	25
THE BUTTERFLY	27
GOOD FOR EVIL	30
THE WREATH OF ROSES	32
LUCY BELL'S DREAM	36
LUCY A THIEF	38
MARY DAY'S SECRET	40
MR. CHARMIN'S SHOP	43

CONTENTS.

	PAGE
THE LOSS	46
THE GUILTY CONSCIENCE	49
THE SCHOOL FEAST	53
THE THUNDER-STORM	57
GEORGE THE GENTLEMAN	62
MARY'S SHOPPING	64
THE GLEANERS	69
THE EARNEST TALK	72
THE MOONLIGHT WALK	76
LUCY'S PRAYER	80
NELLY'S SECRET	84
LUCY AN HONEST GIRL	86
THE DAY OF REST	89
CHRISTMAS EVE	95

THE CHILDREN OF SUMMERBROOK.

SUMMERBROOK.

Away from all the noise and stir
  Of cities and of towns,
A little village lay concealed,
  Amongst the Sussex Downs.

Its history was never writ
  In any learned book;
Few people even knew the name
  Of pleasant Summerbrook.

The houses stood about the fields,
  Or near a winding road,
That skirted now a chalky hill,
  And now a beechen wood.

It passed the school-house and the mill,
  Down to a sunny glen,
Where stood the clustered cottages
  Of many labouring men.

And then with many a pleasant turn,
  Kept on its winding way,
And snug farm-house or mossy cot,
  On either side there lay.

It passed the shop, it crossed the brook,
And by the church it ran,
And there you saw the handsome house,
Of Squire Tyerman.

But we will go into the glen,
So quiet and so fair,
That one would think, Content herself,
Might come and settle there.

At early dawn they heard the dóves,
When all the vale was still,
At eventide the tinkling sound,
Of sheep bells on the hill.

The rooks dwelt in their ancient trees,
The blackbird in the dell,
And there in spring, the nightingale,
His sweet notes warbled well.

And all about, the primroses
Were thick as they could grow,
And pretty little wood-sorrel,
As white as flakes of snow.

The merry children laughed and played,
Beside their cottage door,
And never thought, young happy things,
If they were rich or poor.

The lambs, the birds, the honey-bees,
The squirrels in the wood,
Were all content at Summerbrook;
Were children there, as good?

Dear little people, you for whom,
  I write this story book;
The children were not always good,
  Who lived at Summerbrook.

In truth as far as I could see,
  The children in the Downs,
Were in their hearts exactly like
  The children in the towns.

But if you wish to know them well,
  Then you must come with me,
And I will take you first of all,
  To see good Jenny Lee.

JENNY LEE.

An orphan child was Jenny Lee,
  Her father, he was dead,
And very hard her mother worked,
  To get the children bread.

In winter time, she often rose
  Long ere the day was light,
And left her orphan family,
  Till dark again at night.

And she would always say to Jane,
  Before she went away,
"Be sure you mind the little ones,
  And don't go out to play.

"Keep baby quiet in his bed,
As long as he will lie,
Then take him up, and dance him well,
Don't leave him there to cry.

"And don't let little Christopher,
Get down into the street,
For fear he meets an accident
Beneath the horses' feet.

"And mind about the fire, child,
And keep a tidy floor;
We never need be dirty, Jane,
Although we may be poor.

"Good-bye, my precious comforter,
For all the neighbours say,
That I can trust my little maid,
Whenever I'm away."

Then Jenny she was quite as proud
As England's noble Queen,
And she resolved to do the work,
And keep the dwelling clean.

She did not stop to waste her time,
But very brisk was she;
And worked as hard and cheerfully,
As any busy bee.

If down upon the cottage floor,
Her little brother fell,
She stroked the places tenderly,
And kissed and made them well.

And when the little babe was cross,
As little babes will be,
She nursed and danced it merrily,
And fed it on her knee.

But when they both were safe in bed,
She neatly swept the hearth,
And waited till her mother's step,
Came sounding up the path.

Then open flew the cottage door,
The weary mother smiled;
"Ah! Jenny dear, what should I do,
Without my precious child!"

THE SHEPHERD'S CHILD.

Across the road, just opposite
The house of Jenny Lee,
Another pleasant dwelling stood,
Beneath a chesnut tree.

It was the home of Jesse Miles,
A shepherd on the hill;
His little girl was Katherine,
His wife was often ill.

Young Kitty Miles and Jenny Lee,
Were faithful friends and true,
And helped each other cheerfully,
Though both had much to do.

Before the cock had called the hens,
  That roosted in the shed,
Young Katherine had dressed herself,
  And shaken up her bed.

She threw the window open wide,
  To breathe the morning air,
She washed her round and rosy cheeks,
  And brushed her shining hair.

Then briskly down the stairs she went,
  And when the fire was made,
She swept the room and dusted it,
  And then the breakfast laid.

And up she took a cup of tea,
  And nicely buttered bread,
To tempt her mother's appetite,
  As she lay ill in bed.

She was not loud and boisterous,
  But gently moved and smiled,
You might have fancied her a nurse,
  If you had seen the child.

And when 'twas nearly nine o'clock,
  And Kitty heard the chime,
She put her shawl and bonnet on,
  To be at school in time.

She did not loiter by the way,
  But briskly on she goes,
And if 'twas dirty in the road,
  She tripped upon her toes.

She always was in school the first,
In spite of work or rain;
The mistress then would smile and say,
"Here's Kitty first again!"

And she can nicely write and read,
And neatly hem and sew;
But now I'll tell you what I've heard,
Of little Sally Slow.

THE LAZY GIRL.

Her sister would come to the bedside and call,
"Do you mean to sleep here all the day?
I saw Kitty Miles up two hours ago,
A-washing and working away.

"And I have been milking the old spotted cow,
As she stood by the sycamore tree,
And brought a great handful of Lent lilies home;
That grew on the slope of the lea.

"The water is boiling, the table is spread,
Your father is just at the door;
If you are not quick, we shall eat all the bread,
And you will not find any more."

Then Sally sat up, and half opened her eyes,
And gave both a grunt and a groan,
And yawning, she said, in a quarrelsome voice,
"I wish you would let me alone."

But though she was lazy, she always could eat,
And wished for a plentiful share,
So tumbled her clothes on, and smeared her white face,
Forgetting her hands and her hair.

Her frock was all crumpled and twisted awry,
Her hair was entangled and wild,
Her stockings were down, and her shoes were untied,
She looked a most slovenly child.

She sauntered about, till the old village clock
Had sounded, and then died away,
Before she put on her torn bonnet, and went
To school without further delay.

But soon as she came to the little cake shop,
She loitered with lingering eyes,
Just wishing that she had a penny to spend,
For one of the pretty jam pies.

Again she went on and she loitered again,
In the same foolish way as before,
And the clock in the school, was just warning for ten,
As she lifted the latch of the door.

The governess frowned as she went to her place,
She had spoken so often in vain,
And now only said with a sorrowful sigh,
"There's Sally the latest again!"

She hated her reading and never would write,
She neither could cipher nor sew,
And little girls whispered, "We never will be
So silly as Miss Sally Slow."

THE DIRTY LANE.

Beyond the house of Simon Slow,
There is a narrow lane,
So dirty, that I never wish
To go that way again.

Here lived a man called Joseph Brand,
With Margery his wife,
And such bad management and waste,
I ne'er saw in my life.

There was a puddle at the door,
In which the children played,
And ashes, sticks, and broken pots,
Before the house were laid.

The clothes were hanging on the hedge,
All tattered and torn out,
Not fairly worn and mended up,
But slit and frayed about.

A little rough ill-favoured boy,
Was stamping in the mud,
To make himself from head to foot,
As dirty as he could.

His mother came and caught him there,
And with an angry cuff,
She snatched him up, and then he roared,
And kicked with noise enough.

The other little ragged things,
Were squabbling in the lane;
But as I said, I never wish
To see that place again.

So let us go and see the home,
Of Mr. Andrew White,
Where things as far as I could tell,
Were always going right.

The house stood in a pretty croft,
Where Andrew kept a cow;
And when his orchard was in bloom,
'Twas like a sheet of snow.

The hens and chickens ran about,
The cock crowed on the wall,
The little pond looked quite alive,
With ducklings great and small.

His wife was quiet, clean, and good,
Industrious and kind,
One thought seemed ever uppermost,
In this good woman's mind.

To do to others, as you would
That they should do to you,
This was the thought which Martha White
Kept constantly in view.

She ne'er spoke ill of any one,
 She thought it was not right;
She would not hear of neighbours' faults,
 In that she'd no delight.

But where distress or illness came,
 The people all were sure
That neighbour White would try her best
 To comfort or to cure.

And she could speak with winning words,
 Of God the Saviour's love;
And sometimes led her suffering friends,
 To place their hopes above.

In Summerbrook churchyard there are
 Three small graves in a row,
And on the stone you read the names
 Of those who rest below.

Four little children used to play
 Round Andrew's cottage door;
Now little Nelly plays alone,
 The three play there no more.

Their happy faces in this world
 Will never more be seen;
Their nimble feet will bound no more
 Across the village green.

For they are gone to Paradise,
 Where comes no toil nor pain;
And oh! they would not like to live
 In Summerbrook again.

They sit beneath the Tree of Life,
  Or wander hand in hand,
And sing amongst the lilies,
  In that blessed sunny land.

They talk of little Nelly there,
  And wish her time was come
To leave the house in Summerbrook,
  For their delightsome home.

But Nelly White must stay awhile,
  Until the Lord of love
Shall fit that little tender lamb,
  To dwell with them above.

NELLY WHITE.

The first day Nelly went to school,
  She was but five years old,
A pretty little gentle child,
  And never rude or bold.

She sat upon the lowest form,
  Not far from Lucy Bell,
A girl of more than twelve years old,
  Of whom we've much to tell.

She was not like good Jenny Lee,
  Her words and looks were sour;
And children, if they wanted help,
  Would never come to her.

Now Nelly had not learned to read,
She could not hem or sew,
Nor even thread her needle well,
So little did she know.

And as she sat upon the form,
She tried and tried again,
To thread the needle's little eye,
But still she tried in vain.

At last she said to Lucy Bell,
"My cotton won't go through;
The needle's eye is very small,
I don't know what to do."

"Why! you must do like other girls,
And not be sitting still,
And if it won't go through at first,
Then try it, till it will."

Then Nelly bit the cotton end,
And earnestly she tried;
But always at the little eye,
The cotton slipped aside.

At last the tears rose in her eyes,
And trickled down her face,
And she began to think that school
Was not a happy place.

But very soon she changed her mind,
When smiling Mary Day
Just lifted up her pinafore,
And wiped the tears away.

"What ails you, dear?" she kindly said,
"What is it makes you cry?"
"I cannot make the cotton go
Into the needle's eye."

"And is that all? well give it me,
I soon will set it right;"
And through the eye the cotton went,
Almost as quick as light.

Then Nelly with a happy face,
Some little stitches made,
But then she found a tiresome knot,
Had tangled up her thread.

Her little fingers pulled the knot,
It would not stir for them;
The cotton stuck upon its way,
And would not hem the hem.

"Please Lucy Bell," she softly said,
"Undo this knot for me;"
"Why, child, how troublesome you are!
I wish you'd let me be."

"If you make knots to please yourself,
You must undo them too;
Nor waste the time of other girls,
Who've something else to do."

"Come, give it me," said Mary Day,
"I'll manage it, my dear;"
She soon undid the tiresome knot,
And set the cotton clear.

When Nelly home to dinner went,
  She then began to tell
Her parents about Mary Day,
  And peevish Lucy Bell:

And how the scholars in the school,
  Looked up to Mary Day;
And how when Lucy Bell came near,
  They often ran away.

And Nelly said, "I'll try to be
  As kind as Mary Day,
And not be cross to any one,
  In school time or at play."

Then Andrew praised his little girl,
  And kissed her bonny face,
And said, the Days were all of them,
  A credit to the place.

DANIEL DAY.

A seaman good was Daniel Day,
  A noble British tar,
Who served her Majesty in peace,
  And fought for her in war.

He loved his native country well,
  He gloried in her fame,
And said a true-born Englishman,
  Should guard her honoured name.

But sad was Daniel's manly heart,
When last he left his Jane;
It would be many weary months,
Before they met again.

And she was ill and could not work,
What would she do alone!
How will she bear a life of care,
He thought,—when I am gone?

Then to his children dear, he said,
(George was but twelve years old,)
"Care for your mother, George, my boy,
She's worth her weight in gold.

"And Mary, dear, don't let her want
A loving daughter's care;
And may the Lord reward you both,
That is your father's prayer."

Then Daniel Day, he went away,
To sail upon the sea;
And left to God's protecting care,
His little family.

THE HAPPY HOME.

When first I went to visit Mistress Day,
(Her husband then had been six months away,)
I saw her sitting, as was then her rule,
Watching for Mary till she came from school;

And when she hears her tripping foot so light,
Her face looks cheerful, and her eyes grow bright;
She lays her work upon her knee awhile,
To welcome Mary with a loving smile.
"How are you, mother? I'm afraid you're worse,
Do let me stay at home and be your nurse;
And then perhaps you would get well again,
And not be always in such dreadful pain."
"No, no, dear Mary, that can never be,
You must not grow up ignorant for me;
You'll have to earn your livelihood, you know,
And so must learn betimes to read and sew.
I've had the doctor calling in to day;"
"Oh, have you, mother—and what did he say?"
"He said 'twas little use for him to try,
Unless I gave up work and could lay by;
Were I a lady, he had little fear,
To make me well in less than half a year."
"Did he, indeed—well then, you must be still,
And George and I will work with right good will;
And George has grown a very handy boy,
And always ready for some fresh employ;
It is so good of George, whate'er you ask,
He'll do it as a pleasure, not a task."
As Mary spoke, her brother George came in,
A merry boy with rosy cheeks and chin,
Just twelve years old, and lively as the day,
And quite as ready for his work as play.
He had been whistling as he came along,
Trying to imitate the blackbird's song.

His mother heard him give his music o'er,
And scrape his shoes, beside the cottage door.
"Well, George, my boy"—"Well, mother, how
are you?
You've got some job for me, I guess to do."
But long before his mother made reply,
He caught his sister's quick and speaking eye,
Who through the low-back door in silence passed,
Whilst full on George, a beckoning look she cast.
"Now, George," she said, as soon as he had come,
"I want to speak to you about our home;
The doctor came, and mother's leg he dressed,
And said, he'd cure it, if she could have rest:
Now, brother, I believe that you and I
Could do the work if we were both to try."
"Of course we could, said George, no fear of me,
I'll do my part right well and handsomely;
But we must share the work you know, and take
What suits us best—so, Mary, you must bake;
And you must wash, that's plain enough to tell,
But I will draw the water from the well."
"Yes, Georgy dear, and don't run in the dirt,
Your stockings are so black and so's your shirt,
They take such soap and rubbing to get clean,
To make them white, and proper to be seen."
"Well, you shall see, I'll have another plan,
And be as clean as any gentleman;
Then I will run the errands that you need;
'Tis pretty clear too we must make good speed,
For mother will not have us late at school,

She's such a woman not to break a rule."
"Ah, George, she is a mother!—very few
Have such advantages as I and you.
Oh, how I hope she will get well again;
I cannot bear to see her suffer pain."
"Well, Mary, you and I will do our best,
And if we do the work, then she can rest.
And may perhaps get better, who can tell?
I'd work both day and night to make her well."

This being fixed, these happy children went
To tell their mother what was their intent;
And when they had explained, and made it clear,
And George protested that he had no fear,
She laid a hand upon each youthful head,
And looking in their eager eyes, she said,
"Well, my dear children, you shall have your way,
And do the work for me, and I will play,
And be a lady."—"So you shall indeed,
And we will be your servants, and give heed
To every little thing you may desire;
So now, dear mother, shall we mend the fire,
And put the kettle on and get the tea,
And shew how quick and useful we can be?"

LITTLE PATTY.

As I drew near the house of Mistress Bell,
I heard some words that I'm ashamed to tell.
"I won't," said Lucy, to her mother's call—
"You won't, Miss, won't you? then we'll see—
that's all;
If you don't mind that child—I say again,
I'll tell your father—and you know what then."
And then, I saw (of course I was not seen,)
Lucy come out, I don't know where she'd been;
But she came forward with a crawling pace,
Just like a snail—and such a sulky face;
She muttered something—and then tossed her head,
I did not understand the words she said;
But I could see she hated to obey,
And meant if possible to get her way.
A little child was just outside the door,
Playing with dust, and wanted nothing more;
For though she was too dirty to be seen,
She was as happy as a little queen.
She kicked the dust and shook her curly head,
Laughing to see the smother she had made;
But when she saw her sister drawing nigh,
She puckered up her little face to cry.
"What are you doing there?—a pretty sight!
How dare you make yourself in such a plight?"
She snatched the frightened infant by the hand,
And plucked her up, and roughly bid her stand.

"Look what you've done! I'll whip you, Miss, right well,
You naughty child, I will," said Lucy Bell.
And then she shook and slapped the little thing,
And by the sound, I'm sure the slap would sting;
Then rudely pushed and sharply jerked her round,
Of course again she fell upon the ground.
"Now, can't you stand?—I'll teach you how to play,
And make yourself this mess another day!
And if you cry, I'll call the sweep to come;
The black old man to take you to his home."
The frightened child clung close to Lucy's side,
But vainly tried its swelling sobs to hide.
Poor little Patty was but three years old,
And knew not how her childish grief to hold;
And sobbing, Lucy dragged her up the road,
Threat'ning to whip her if she was not good.

The case was this, that Lucy Bell had planned,
To steal away to walk with Susan Brand.
So, when her mother wanted her to stay
To mind the child, she wished to disobey;
But still she would not have her father know,
For he could give a very heavy blow,
Which Lucy felt sometimes, and was afraid
Her mother's promise was too truly made.
Now Mistress Bell she ruled her house by fear,
Scolding or beating you might always hear;
And as the children grew, they did the same,
Had little love, and very little shame;

And thus you hear of Lucy's cruel spite
To little Patty in her dirty plight.
But let me ask each little girl by name,
Have you been so unkind, and done the same?
Make answer to yourself, quite true and plain,
And if you have, then don't do so again.
I think I hear you say, you would not be
Like Lucy Bell for all that you could see.
Well there she is, and now we see her stand
Upon the road, and there is Susan Brand.
She had been waiting long to join her friend,
And little thinking how their walk would end.
"Why have you brought the child? she cannot go!
If you take her you'll have to walk so slow!"
"I could not help it.—We will leave her here,
We sha'nt be long, and there's no danger near."
Then threatening Patty, if she dared to stir,
She set her on the bank, and left her there;
And both the girls jumped o'er a gate close by,
Glad to escape, and laughing heartily.
Frightened to find itself left all alone,
The child began to scream when they were gone.
Fearing to see the black old man come by—
She did not know that Lucy told a lie;
Afraid to stir, afraid to look or peep,
She sobbed and sobbed, until she fell asleep.
Surely 'tis cruel—wicked, if you please,
To frighten children with such tales as these.
As the poor infant near the footpath lay,
Mary and George came trudging home that way;

They'd been to shop, to buy their weekly store,
And a great basket they between them bore.
They stopped, surprised to find the child out there,
And not to see her sister anywhere;
So Mary carried little Patty home,
And told her brother she would quickly come.
Now Mistress Bell was much displeased indeed,
And would not hear a word that Lucy said;
She told her father as she said she would,
And he beat Lucy, but it did no good;
For when the beating and the pain were o'er,
She grew more hardened then she was before.
So now, dear children, you have heard me tell,
Of this sad visit unto Mistress Bell.

THE CROSS GIRLS.

The school was closed one afternoon,
  And all the girls were gone;
Some walked away in company,
  And some walked on alone.

Some plucked the flowers upon the banks,
  Some chattered very fast,
And some were talking secretly,
  And whispered as you passed.

And if, perchance, a girl came near,
  Then one of these would say,
"Don't listen to our secrets, Miss,
  You'll please to go away."

As Nelly White ran home from school,
  Her work-bag in her hand;
She came close up to Lucy Bell,
  And her friend Susan Brand.

"We don't want you," said Lucy Bell,
  You little tiresome chit;
Our secrets are not meant for you,
  You little Tell-tale-tit."

Then both the girls cried "Tell-tale-tit,"
  And pushed her roughly by;
Poor Nelly said, "I'm no such thing,"
  And then began to cry.

She walked on slowly by herself,
  Then heard a footstep near;
And turning round, was glad to see
  Kind Mary Day appear.

"Well, what's the matter, little Nell?
  You look so dull to day;
Come walk with me and tell me all,
  And wipe these tears away."

"I can't bear Lucy Bell at all,
  She is so cross to me;
And I shall not be kind to her,
  And that I'll let her see."

"Oh, Nell, that is a foolish way,
  You'll be as bad as she;
If you are cross and she is cross,
  You never will agree.

"If she is cross, you must be kind,
That is the only way;
And if you do but persevere,
She may be kind some day."

"I'm sure I wish she would be kind,
And that friend Susan too;
Dear Mary Day, do take my part,
And tell me what to do."

"Well then, if you'll take my advice,
We soon will let them see,
That we can still be kind to them,
However cross they be."

"Yes, so we will, if you will help,
I shall not mind them then,
And if they call me "Tell-tale-tit,"
I will not speak again."

'Twas thus they parted on that day,
Resolving to do right;
And very proud of her good friend,
Was little Nelly White.

THE BUTTERFLY.

As Mary Day and Nelly White
Went off to school next day,
The morning sun was shining bright,
And every thing was gay.

The dew was sparkling on the grass,
The lark was in the sky;
And dancing on before them went
A yellow butterfly.

"Oh! let us catch it, Mary, do,
I'll try and beat it down;
See now! 'tis settled on that leaf,
Ah! silly thing, 'tis gone."

"Oh! Nelly, pray don't beat it down,
You'll hurt the little thing;
Why should you want to catch it, dear?
You'll spoil its pretty wing."

"I never thought that it would feel,
Or suffer any pain;
But if you really think it will,
I won't do so again.

"But are you sure they can be hurt,
As much as you and I;
Such things as beetles, frogs, and toads,
And little things that fly?"

"I'm very sure they suffer pain,
How much I cannot say;
But I can't bear to have them hurt,
Or see them run away.

"Beside they live so happily,
If they are let alone;
They never wish to trouble us,
Nor injure any one.

"I often watch them at their work,
And feel such great surprise,
That such small creatures as they are,
Should be so very wise."

"Well, I should like to watch them too,
To see how wise they are."
"Then just look at this cobweb, made
By that small spider there."

"That nasty spider! you don't mean
To say that he is wise!"
"Dear Nelly, watch a little bit,
And try and use your eyes.

"See, how he draws his thread along,
That's finer than a hair,
And seems to join it with a touch,
At every little square.

"And look how very fast he works,
And yet the work is strong,
And though he never has been taught,
He never does it wrong.

"He has no pattern there to show,
Where he should draw his thread;
The pattern and the working too,
Are in his little head."

"How did it get into his head?
I wonder if you know."
"Yes; God who made him put it there,
But I can't tell you how.

"I only know they're always right,
And never go astray;
And all the work they have to do,
Is done the neatest way.

"Whilst you and I are often wrong,
And many a blunder make;
A little spider weaves a web,
Without the least mistake.

"My mother says that we may learn,
From e'en the smallest thing,
That all God's creatures every where,
A useful lesson bring."

But now they're at the school-room door,
And soon they take their place;
And many girls looked pleased to see
Dear Mary's happy face.

GOOD FOR EVIL.

"Bring up your slates," the mistress said,
"And all stand up in class,
The cipherers may come to me,
The second class may parse."

Then with their slates, and pencils sharp,
The scholars gathered round;
But Lucy Bell was looking down
For something on the ground.

"Come, Lucy Bell, what makes you stay?"
The Mistress looked severe;
"The class is waiting here for you,
We have no time to spare."

"I've lost my pencil, Ma'am," said she.
"Yes—that is just your way,
And I shall punish you this time,
And keep you in from play.

"I have to find more fault with you,
Than any girl in school,
And if you do not come at once,
You'll stand up on the stool."

With reddened cheeks, she once more turned
Her work-bag inside out;
The pencil was not to be found,
And she began to pout.

That moment a most happy thought
Came into Nelly's mind;
"She shall have my slate-pencil now,
For that is being kind."

And so she softly left her place,
And went to Lucy Bell;
"Here is my pencil, if you like,
Perhaps 'twill do as well."

Then Lucy snatched it from her hand,
And went and took her place;
But never once thanked Nelly White,
Who saved her from disgrace.

The friends met after school again,
As they had done before;
And hand in hand together walked,
As far as Nelly's door.

"Well, Mary, did you see how good
I was to Lucy Bell?
I am so glad I thought of it,
So glad, I cannot tell.

"But she was rough, and did not smile,
Nor even 'thank you,' say;
She snatched the pencil from my hand,
And quickly turned away."

"Well, Nelly, never care for that,
You know you have been kind,
And so you may be satisfied,
One day she'll change her mind."

THE WREATH OF ROSES.

"I'll tell you what I mean to do,"
Said Lucy to her friend;
"I've been to Charmin's shop to day,
Just at the village end.

"You should have seen how splendidly
The window was set out,
And how the ribbons and the gowns,
Were hung and spread about!

"But oh! the flowers, I never saw
Such beauties as they had;
If I can't get some for myself,
'Twill almost drive me mad.

"The thing I long for is a wreath
Of rose-buds, white and red;
I asked the man the lowest price,
And what do you think he said?"

"Perhaps 'twas sixpence, I don't know."
"I see you do not, Sue;
Why, child, 'twas just as much again,
And quite a bargain too!

"I've set my mind to get that wreath,
But how, I do not know;
I'll turn it over in my head,
And manage it somehow.

"I am to have a lovely frock,
With flounces, and *so* wide,
And that will be made up, you know,
In time for Whitsuntide.

"It is the sweetest light sky-blue,
Just fit for summer wear;
And I'm to have a ribbon sash!
Yes, Susan, you may stare!

"And I'm to have a bonnet too,
With *little* strings to tie;
And on each side a small rosette,
And ribbon strings to fly.

"Then if I get that rose-bud wreath,
And just a little lace,
It will become me very much;
The colour suits my face.

"And little Pat will be so fine,
You'll hardly know her, Sue,
For she's to have a new white frock,
And handsome trowsers too.

"My mother says the frock won't come
Quite down to Patty's knee;
And so the work and little tucks
Will all be shown, you see.

"I mean to make myself some sleeves,
Like Nancy at the hall;
And she has worked a collar too,
A petticoat and all.

"I do delight in fancy work,
I hate to hem and sew;
If I could choose I would not set
Another stitch, I know.

"My mother likes to see us smart,
She'd count it quite a shame,
To go to church like somebody,
That you and I could name."

Then both the girls laughed heartily,
And joked at Mary Day;
"A little prim, old-fashioned thing,"
The worst that they could say.

"But how you ever get such clothes,
I cannot understand!
I wish that I could have the chance,
I know," said Susan Brand.

"My father scolds in such a way,
If mother goes on trust;
But if we bought such handsome clothes,
Of course you know we must.

"He says, that useful decent things,
Are all that he can stand;
That finery and beggary
Go mostly hand in hand.

"Now wife," says he, "I charge you well,
Don't get a beggar's name;
Fine clothes and drinking are the things
That bring a man to shame."

"He talked of that fine feather too,
In little Patty's hat;
And said, 'You'll see that Mrs. Bell
Will *beg* to pay for that.'"

"Perhaps your father may be right,
Perhaps he may be wrong;
But I don't care for that, I'll have
My wreath, before 'tis long."

LUCY BELL'S DREAM.

The latest thought of Lucy Bell,
As she lay down that night,
Was how to get the pretty wreath
Of rose-buds, red and white.

When Lucy's eyes were closed in sleep,
And all were gone to bed,
In dreams she still distinctly saw,
The rose-buds, white and red.

The door was locked, the shutters closed,
And very dark the night,
But still the wreath of pretty buds,
Was always in her sight.

When Mistress Bell woke in the night,
She heard her daughter say,
"Oh! they have got the pretty wreath,
And taken it away."

"A foolish child," said Mistress Bell,
"She's dreaming now of that,
But she can't have it, I'm in debt
For Patty's tuscan hat.

"For Lucy's frock, and bonnet too,
And several little things;
Beside, I want a Sunday cap,
As well as bonnet strings.

" And Charmin spoke quite short to day,
  About my small account;
And said he wasn't warranted,
  To add to the amount.

" I can't say that I see just how,
  The payment will be met;
But that will come another day,
  I shall not pay him yet.

" I hope my Jem won't get to know,
  I must take care of that;
He thinks I earned the cash to pay
  For Patty's tuscan hat."

'Twas very long ere Mistress Bell,
  These anxious thoughts could still;
And when she went to sleep again,
  She dreamt about the bill.

LUCY A THIEF.

How brightly does the morning sun,
Shine down upon the earth;
To waken every living thing,
To gratitude and mirth.

The sweet fresh air is all astir,
To scatter rosy health;
And brings it to the working man,
As well as man of wealth.

But at the door of Mistress Bell,
No welcome could it win;
For though it was so bright without,
There was a cloud within.

'Twas Lucy's plan to fret and tease,
And now it was her thought,
That if she teased and sulked enough,
The roses would be bought.

But Lucy was mistaken here,
The bill was still to pay;
And angrily her mother said,
She'd take her sash away.

So Lucy Bell went off to school,
Exclaiming with a frown,
"I will contrive some way, I will,
To get it for my own."

She did not care about her work,
She lost her place in class,
The wreath was plain before her eyes,
As in a looking glass.

"Are you asleep?" the Mistress said,
"What makes you blunder so?
You cannot say your tasks at all,
Not one of them you know!"

Now Lucy's place upon the form
Was next to Mary Day;
And Mary left her work-bag there,—
Upon the desk it lay.

Then Lucy took it carelessly,
And just undrew the string,
And saw a silver shilling there,
Said she, "That's just the thing!"

And almost ere an eye could wink,
Or e'en her thought be known,
She whipped it out of Mary's bag,
And popped it in her own.

"There now—I'll buy that charming wreath!
The price will just be right;"
And then her face turned very red,
And then turned very white.

MARY DAY'S SECRET.

"I wonder what you're going to buy,
Do tell me, Mary, dear;
If 'tis a secret, I won't tell,
I should so like to hear."

"Well, Nelly, no one knows it yet,
But I will trust to you;
There are not many girls I'd tell,
But you speak always true."

"Then, tell me first, how you could get,
A shilling for to spend?
You may be sure I shall not tell,
Because I am you friend."

"I've earned it all at different times,
You soon may do the same;
I hemmed some pocket handkerchiefs,
And marked them with the name.

"And I have sometimes cleaned the school,
And one or two things more;
So, Nelly, you may plainly see,
How I have made my store."

"Well, shall you buy some gingerbread,
Or puffs—they are so nice;
Or oranges, or peppermint,
Or cakes of licorice?"

"No; nothing of that kind at all,
  The taste so soon is past;
I mean to lay my money out
  In something that will last."

"Then, shall you buy some pretty clothes,
  A collar or a bow;
Or pretty pink silk handkerchief,
  Like Lucy Bell's, you know?"

Then Mary laughed out heartily,
  And slackening her pace;
Took little Nelly by the hand,
  And looking in her face,

Said—"Now I'll tell you, Nelly, dear,
  Because we're friends, you see;
And when you have a secret too,
  Why, you can tell it me."

"Yes; that I will," said Nelly White,
  "I wish I had one now;
But come, do tell me, what you'll buy,
  I want so much to know."

Then Mary Day looked round to see
  If any one was near;
And only spoke out loud enough
  For Nelly White to hear.

"Well; I've two sixpences to spend;
  With one, I mean to buy
A present for my brother George,—
  A pretty blue neck-tie.

"And with the other, I intend
(Because I've been to see,)
To buy a little tea-caddy,
To hold my mother's tea."

"I know she does so wish to have
A tidy little box;
And there is one of black japan,
And more than that—it locks!"

"But then, what will you have yourself?"
Said little Nelly White;
"Oh! I shall have the fun, you know,
Of seeing their delight.

"I just can see my brother George,
He'll laugh and jump and shout,
And say, 'There's no one like our Poll
The country round about.'

"And then my mother she will smile,
And give me such a kiss;
Oh! Nell, no puffs nor peppermint,
Could be so sweet as this."

"I should so like to go with you,
To see the things you buy;
And I can bring the pretty box,
And you the blue neck-tie."

"Well, so you shall, but let's make haste,
We have no time to stop;"
And so they skipped along the road
To Mr. Charmin's shop.

MR. CHARMIN'S SHOP.

The little girls set off and did not stop,
Till they arrived at Mr. Charmin's shop;
And as you do not know it, I will try,
To tell you something of its history.
For many years this shop had been the place
Where all the working people bought their dress;
Their grocery; their pots and pans; their cheese,
Butter, and treacle, bacon, flour, and peas,
Matches, and shot, tin-ware, and balls of string;
A little, one might say, of every thing.
Small store of each, because the shop was small,
But still for years, it quite contented all;
It was nine miles to reach the nearest town,
And few went there to buy a cap or gown.
But just twelve months before the time I write,
The village people saw a wondrous sight;
The little low shop front had given place
To one, three times the size, of fine plate glass;
And the small parlour at the back, was laid
Into the shop, to suit a larger trade.
Then off to London Mr. Charmin went,
To buy a stock for taste and ornament;
And when the window was in full display,
It was as fine as tulip beds in May;
And wives and maidens, wondering at the sight,
Gave up their senses to a new delight.

Some aged people, by experience wise,
Looked at the matter with regretful eyes;
And said, that decent clothes would soon give place
To flowers and fringes, parasols and lace.
There were two things, which spoiled a poor man's life—
Drink for himself, and dressing for his wife;
They shook their heads, whene'er they had to pass,
Foreboding ill to many a village lass.
Oh dear! how all the little girls did stop,
To feast their eyes at Mr. Charmin's shop.
They loved the ribbons, all, except the brown,
And how they wished they'd money of their own.
So many pretty things they'd like to buy,
To make themselves a heap of finery.
Then off they ran to school, afraid to stay,
And talked about the ribbons all the way.
To elder girls, it was a greater snare,
Full half their thoughts were sure to wander there;
And more than half their talk whene'er they met,
Concerned the handsome things they meant to get.
A book of fashions in the window laid,
A charming book to every village maid.
When the young servant on an errand went,
To Charmin's shop her steps were often bent,
To ask the price of something, or to buy
Some tempting bit of useless finery;
Or read the fashion book to get a hint,
To make the sleeve, or body of her print.

Then hastening home, and questioned, why delayed,
A ready falsehood often came to aid.
'Twas odd to see, how very soon arose
A call for dressmakers to make the clothes.
Before the fashion book had come to town,
Mothers and daughters always made their own;
But now, not e'en the sharpest could detect
The proper *cut*, to give the right effect.
Thus in the space of just twelve months, or less,
Town hands found work in making village dress.
And some gave up—for instance, Mistress Bell—
To wash at home, she could not iron well:
And flounces must be stiff and well set out,
Or else they draggle down, or cling about.
So, whilst the love of finery increased,
Home comforts dwindled to the very least;
And household management grew worse and worse,
And debts increased upon an empty purse.
For as the wages kept the same, of course
The under-clothing, and the fare were worse;
And children staid from school, for want of pence,
And thus grew up in shameful ignorance;
And others walked with bold undaunted eye,
To shew their clothes to every passer by.
All would be fine; the passion grew apace,
The dirtiest girl had flowers about her face,
Mixed in with gaudy bows and dingy strings,
The most unsightly, of unsightly things;
But there were consequences, worse than these,
Some other day, I'll tell you, if you please.

I don't believe the words so often said,
That all this finery is good for trade;
But my long history must have a stop,
For now we're all at Mr. Charmin's shop.

THE LOSS.

The shop was full as usual,
  So Mary had to wait,
And felt a little anxious too,
  For fear they should be late.

"I'll get my money out," she said,
  "And when my turn is come,
I know the things I mean to buy,
  And then we'll scamper home.

"There stands the caddy on the shelf,
  There's George's tie, you see."
And little Nelly clapped her hands,
  And jumped about with glee.

They stood just at the counter's end,
  Not far from Lucy Bell;
And saw her looking at a wreath,
  The wreath she loved so well.

Then Mary Day undrew her bag,
  To take the shilling out;
But soon the whole contents were turned,
  And scattered all about.

"My shilling's gone! it is not here,
  Oh dear! where can it be;
I must have lost it on the road,
  Do let us run and see."

Away they went, with eager eyes,
  Examining the road;
Now running here, now running there;
  Alas! it was no good.

But still they hunted up and down,
  And up and down again;
We all know where the shilling was,
  And that the search was vain.

At last e'en little Nelly talked
  In sad despairing tones;
But still she looked among the grass,
  And even moved the stones.

"Oh! here comes Lucy Bell," she said,
  "Sure now—she can't be cross;"
And off she ran to Lucy Bell,
  To tell of Mary's loss.

And such a piteous history
  She made of Mary's case;
Whilst all the time the sparkling tears,
  Were rolling down her face;

That even Lucy Bell looked grieved,
But said she could not stay;
Though Nelly begged she'd help to look,
Before she went away.

"Well, we must give it up for lost,"
Said Mary with a sigh;
"I did so wish to please them both;"
And she began to cry.

And freely ran the trickling tears,
Upon her mournful face;
She was not crying for herself,
And so, 'twas no disgrace.

"Poor mother will not have her box,
Nor George his nice neck-tie;
But 'tis no use to fret, I know,
So Nelly, dear, good-bye."

And all these little girls went home;
Which would you be, I pray—
Proud Lucy, with her stolen wreath,
Or weeping Mary Day?

THE GUILTY CONSCIENCE.

'Twas very long ere Lucy Bell,
Could get to sleep that night;
For just as she began to doze,
She woke up in affright.

And when she slept, she started oft,
Then fetched a heavy sigh;
And dreamed that something had been lost,
And heard poor Mary cry.

If Lucy's mother had been there,
And watching at her side;
She might have learned the very thing,
That Lucy wished to hide.

For Lucy dreamt that she was caught,
And then she gave a scream;
No one can tell what they may say,
When they are in a dream.

And as she at her breakfast sat,
Upon the morrow morn,
She scarcely said a word, but seemed
Dejected and forlorn.

At last her mother spoke, and said,
"What is the matter, child?
'Twas but a day or two ago,
That you were nearly wild;

"Because the day was close at hand,
When all the scholars meet
At Squire Tyerman's, at the hall,
To have the yearly treat.

"I can't think what has happened now,
To make you look so dull;
Your clothes I'm sure are to your mind,
They're very beautiful.

"I know that not a scholar there,
Will look so well as you;"
But at each word her mother spoke,
More gloomy Lucy grew:

Still said, she was not dull at all,
Though she was fit to cry;
So very close upon a theft,
Is sure to hang a lie.

"How came you by that pretty wreath?"
Again, said Mistress Bell;
And Lucy said 'twas given her,
Oh! Lucy—Lucy Bell!

And then afraid, that she might have
To answer something more,
She said, 'twas time to go to school,
And started from the door.

And as she went along the road,
She was in great affright,
Lest she should see poor Mary Day,
Or little Nelly White.

There was a terror on her mind,
  She could not drive away;
She made mistakes in all her work;
  She did not care to play.

The wicked thing that she had done,
  Lay on her heart like lead;
When people spoke, her colour changed,
  And down she hung her head.

But most of all she feared to meet
  The eye of Mary Day;
And at each turn she tried to keep
  Quite out of Mary's way.

And when the school broke up, she chose
  To walk away alone;
She had a secret now, she dare
  Not tell to any one.

Some girls came up to her and said,
  "Why! this is something new;
What is the matter, Lucy Bell?"
  Said she, "What's that to you?"

And when they talked about the feast,
  She scarcely spoke at all;
She felt afraid to shew her wreath
  To-morrow at the hall.

So passed the day—a heavy day,
  And as the night drew on,
She started up at every sound,
  She feared to be alone.

For still the deed that she had done,
Lay on her heart like lead;
And when her mother spoke to her,
She scarcely raised her head.

"Come, tell me now about that wreath!
For I must know it all;"
And Lucy said, "'Twas given her,
By Nancy, at the hall."

Now Nancy was a dressy girl,
And Lucy's cousin too;
So Mistress Bell was satisfied,
And thought the tale was true.

She took the wreath, and pinned it in,
And said, "Look! that is nice;"
But Lucy shivered as she looked,
She felt as cold as ice.

How peacefully good children sleep!
Who nothing wrong have done;
They're not afraid to speak the truth,
Nor fear to be alone.

And when dear Mary Day had prayed
Her prayer beside her bed;
She lay down happily to sleep,
No trouble filled her head.

For that great God, who made us all,
Who rules the earth and sky,
Keeps every good and praying child
Beneath his watchful eye.

THE SCHOOL FEAST.

The thrush sung loud, the lark rose high,
  It was a glorious morn;
The dew-drops hung like diamonds,
  Upon the springing corn.

The sun rode through the clear blue sky,
  No cloud was sailing there,
And sunshine lay on all the flowers,
  And sweetness filled the air.

And bright young eyes from cottage doors,
  Looked out upon the sight;
And glad young hearts were beating fast,
  Forestalling their delight.

And busy hands up at the Hall,
  Were cutting piles of cake,
And called on all, both great and small,
  Some work to undertake.

And so the hours flew quickly by
  Until the afternoon;
And then with flag and flageolet,
  And fiddle and bassoon,

The children marched up to the Hall,
  All in their best array,
And every face, excepting one,
  Was satisfied and gay.

Some games had kindly been contrived,
The merry hours to pass;
They played at ball and races ran,
Upon the level grass.

Some children played at blindman's-buff,
Some swung upon a tree;
Until 'twas time to sing the grace,
And then sit down to tea.

'Twas wonderful to see the lumps
The little ones would take;
And what an appetite they had
For Squire Tyerman's cake.

The tea went round, the buttered bread,
Then cake again was tried;
Till every little hungry child
Was fully satisfied.

Then off again they went to play,
Or walk about the grounds;
And gentlefolks who came to tea,
They also took the rounds.

A gentleman and lady walked,
Through all the happy band;
And children smiled and curtsied low,
To pretty Mistress Bland.

And as they passed by Mary Day,
The gentleman spoke low—
"There, that's the girl, you'd like to nurse
Your little Maud, I know."

"That very thought," the lady said,
"Was passing through my mind;
The sweetest face I ever saw,
So modest and so kind."

"We'll ask her if she wants a place;"
And then without delay,
He asked the question pleasantly,
Of gentle Mary Day.

"When mother's better, sir, I shall,"
She said with blushing face;
"Well, then, you'll come to Mistress Bland,
And ask her for a place."

He put a shilling in her hand,
And smiling then, he said,
"There, now you see, I've hired you
To be our little maid."

Then walking on they joined a group,
Where Lucy Bell was queen,
And there she stood dressed out so fine,
Expecting to be seen.

"How different!" the lady said,
"What foolish airs she has,
Do, Harry, dear, observe that girl,
Do just look at her dress!"

"Oh! she's not worth a second look,
So tawdry and so vain;
I like that little rosy girl,
Who dressed so neat and plain."

"That smart girl's mother came to beg
  Last winter at our door;
And such a dismal tale she told,
  I thought them very poor."

"Aye, Fanny, dear," the husband said,
  "You've yet to understand,
That finery and beggary
  Go often hand in hand."

Just as he spoke, he felt a drop,
  And looked up in the sky,
"The clouds are gathering fast," he said,
  A thunder-storm is nigh."

Then off he went with quickened step,
  The little girls to call,
And told them all to hasten home,
  Before the rain should fall.

Away they ran in haste, pell-mell,
  Their different homes to find;
And in less time than you would think,
  Not one was left behind.

THE THUNDER-STORM.

The first large drops fell wide apart,
Like those of summer heat,
And seemed as if they'd not the heart,
To spoil the children's treat.

Thus many girls, whose homes were near
Squire Tyerman's at the hall,
Just reached their parents' doors before
The rain began to fall.

But Lucy Bell and Mary Day
Had full a mile to go,
And partly through the standing corn,
And by the tall hedge-row.

Now Lucy started off at once,
She thought about her dress;
And as she'd but a parasol,
She felt no small distress.

But Mary stopped to pin the frocks
Of many little friends;
And ere she reached the outer gate,
The heavy rain descends.

But having pinned her tippet tight,
And turned her frock up high;
Her large umbrella sheltered her,
And kept her nearly dry.

Still fast and faster fell the rain,
  It dropped from off the trees,
And suddenly the quiet air,
  Sprung up into a breeze.

It blew the slender corn about,
  Through which she had to pass,
And scattered showers of rain-drops down,
  Upon the heavy grass.

Still fast, and faster fell the rain,
  It was a tempest shower,
And Mary now distinctly heard
  The distant thunder roar.

But on she went, she did not fear
  To hear the thunder roar;
And now she saw poor Lucy Bell,
  A little way before.

Her parasol, too small to shield,
  From either rain or sun,
Was dripping now from every point;
  Far better had she none.

Her flying ribbons, late so gay,
  Hung down in dabbled strings,
The colour run and smudged about,
  Most miserable things!

The flounces of her dress were soaked,
  Much higher than her knee;
And such a dirty draggle-tail,
  'Twas pitiful to see.

"Stop, stop," said Mary, "till I come,
For I can shelter you;
My large umbrella here, you see,
Is big enough for two."

Poor Lucy sobbed just like a child,
She was in such a plight,
And still more vexed that Mary Day
Should come and see the sight.

For Mary's kind and friendly voice,
Increased her inward shame.
"I do not want to have her help,
I'd rather have her blame."

But Mary knew not Lucy's thoughts,
And would not be denied,
So held the large umbrella still,
Quite over Lucy's side.

"My frock is only print, she said,
And so it will not hurt;
But yours I doubt will never wash,
To clean it from the dirt.

"'Twas such a pity that you came
So early from the feast,
I might have kept you almost dry,
Your bonnet at the least.

Your pretty flowers are almost spoiled,
And those nice ribbon strings."
"Oh! I don't care about the flowers;
I hate the nasty things."

As Mary did not know the cause,
Nor could a reason find;
She only thought 'twas Lucy's way,
When things weren't to her mind.

So then she talked about the treat
They'd had up at the hall;
And Lucy said, 'twas very dull,
She was not pleased at all.

Then Mary talked of other things,
Still guarding Lucy's dress;
Until her proud and stubborn heart,
Was melted to confess.

"How kind," she said, "you are to me!"
And sighed a heavy sigh;
"I'm sure *I* had no right to think
That *you* would keep me dry."

"Why not?" said Mary, and she looked
At Lucy with surprise;
And Lucy looked upon the ground,
She dared not raise her eyes.

"What made you think that I should be
So spiteful and unkind?
I'm sorry that I had to stay
So very long behind."

"Oh! don't be sorry—'tis not that—
I did not think of spite—
If you had left me in the rain,
You would have served me right.

"I don't deserve a thought from you"—
And Lucy gasped for breath—
"Oh, Mary! it was I who took
Your shilling for this wreath.

"I have not had a moment's peace,
Since I saw you and Nell;
I've wished it back a thousand times,
But then I dare not tell.

"I'm sure you never can forgive
The wicked thing I've done;
But pray don't let the others know,
Nor yet tell any one."

"I won't, indeed," said Mary Day,
"You need not have a fear."
"Then you're an angel, that is all,
I always knew you were."

But now they're come to Lucy's door,
And there they bid farewell.
"If I don't copy Mary Day,
My name's not Lucy Bell."

GEORGE THE GENTLEMAN.

George was the prince of boys! morn, noon, or
night,
Whate'er he had to do, 't was always right;
No murmur, nor excuses, nor debate,
That 'twas too early, or it was too late;
For when by George his mother's will was known,
In little time, his mother's will was done.
And as to Mary, that dear girl, and he,
Were just as happy as they well could be.
"Our little Polly," was the name she bore,
And when her brother heard her at the door,
He went like any Squire of the land,
And took the wet umbrella from her hand,
And changed her shoes, and gently shook her
dress,
Till Mary laughed at George's carefulness,
And gave him such a kiss, as sisters can,
And said, "Ah! George, you are a gentleman!"
"And how's dear mother?" "Oh, she's charmingly,
We've been so merry, Polly, she and I.
She says, she has not half the pain she had,
And that her leg is nothing like so bad;
So there's encouragement for you and me,
To persevere and go on steadily."
"And I declare, George, I have seen this week,
That she has quite a colour on her cheek."

"She's beautiful," said George; "oh, trust to me,
We'll have her strong, when father comes from sea;
We've still some months; that gives a famous chance,
If, as she says, she always makes advance;
And that she shall, if we can have our way,
I think such work is just as good as play."
I think so too; and Father *will* be glad;
When last he left us, he was very sad,
And how he charged us to be kind and good,
And begged us both to help her all we could."
"And so we have, and so we will, and then,
Mary you know, he'll trust us both again;
That's what I like, it makes one feel so pleased,
Instead of being scolded, snubbed and teased,
Like young Tom Bell; there's always such a noise:"
"Yes, George; but he's the very worst of boys."
"Well, so he is, but he's not all to blame;
If I'd his mother, I should be the same;
You can't think how they quarrel and go on,
I'm finely glad that I am not her son:
For *little* things she always chides him so,
But when he's really wrong, she lets it go."
"I pity Lucy," Mary said, and sighed.
"Well, pray don't mention her," young George replied,
"The most unpleasant girl all round about;
Were you like her, we should be falling out."

And then George laughed, as if 't were possible,
That Mary Day should be like Lucy Bell.
And so they sat, and chatted for awhile,
Till Mary said, with a mysterious smile,
"I have a little business of my own
I wish to do, before our mother's down,
And want to get beforehand with my work;
So when you wake, if't is a little dark,
Do call me, George."—"A secret, Mary, hey?"
"Now do not question, brother George, I pray,
You'll know in time;" and Mary shook her head,
And lit the candle, and went up to bed.

MARY'S SHOPPING.

Full many times, I've heard it said,
I do not say 'tis true,
That children's money has a trick
Of burning pockets through.

But whether it be true or not,
'Tis certain Mary Day
Lay planning in her bed that night,
To pay her own away.

And long before her brother George
  Came tapping at the door,
She'd cleaned the grate and lit the fire,
  And swept the kitchen floor.

For Mary had made up her mind,
  To go without delay,
To buy the caddy and the tie,
  Upon that very day.

She set the kettle on to boil,
  And then she did not stop;
But with a light and bounding step,
  Set off to Charmin's shop.

The morning air was calm and sweet,
  Refreshed by tempest showers;
And heavy lay the glistening dew,
  Upon the grass and flowers.

A light mist from the meadows rose,
  Drawn upward to the sky;
And every bush and leafy tree,
  Was full of melody.

And Mary sometimes checked her pace,
  To try if she could see
What little birds they were that sung
  So sweetly in the tree.

"How beautiful it is!" she said,
  And raised her beaming eyes,
And turned her honest rosy face
  Full upward to the skies.

And God, who fills the earth and sky,
  Looked down on Mary there;
And as she walked along the way,
  His Spirit walked with her,

And filled her heart brim-full of love
  To every creature round;
She could not for the world have hurt
  An insect on the ground.

A bright green beetle, burnished gold,
  Ran swiftly o'er the road;
"You pretty little thing," she said,
  "I'm sure you must be good."

The bees hummed on from flower to flower,
  To sip the fragrant dew;
"You clever, little busy bees,
  I'm not so wise as you."

A rabbit next sprung o'er the path,
  To gain the nearest shade;
"You little darling dear, she said,
  You need not be afraid:"

"I would not hurt you for the world,
  Nor shoot you with a gun;
Not even though you eat our peas,
  You little hungry one."

And then she said, "Poor Lucy Bell,
  How sorry she must be!
I'll never tell to any one
  The secret she told me.

"If I had not been better taught,
I might have done just so;
And I am sure I should not like
That any one should know.

"I wish her mother was like mine,
How happy she might be;
I'll ask my mother, if I may
Invite her in to tea,

"And then perhaps she'd speak to her,
And give her good advice;
And if she grew a better girl,
Oh dear, that would be nice!"

So Mary Day talked to herself,
And wanted no replies;
But when she thought of Lucy Bell,
The tears rose in her eyes.

At last, before the fine shop door
She makes a sudden stop;
She is the earliest customer
At Mr. Charmin's shop.

He soon brought out the very things
That Mary came to buy;
But wished to know how *she* could want
A caddy and a tie?

He liked to talk to Mary Day,
He said she'd turn out well,
And she was very ready too,
Her errand there to tell.

What Mr. Bland had given her,
  And what she meant to do,
And what a great surprise 't would be
  To George and mother too.

"That's right, my little maid," said he,
  And gave her chin a chuck,
Then filled the caddy full of tea,
  And said, "it was for luck."

I need not tell you, then, how fast
  She ran to reach her home;
Lest she should find her mother down,
  Or George to breakfast come.

She is in time—he is not in,
  Her mother is not there;
So, quick she took her bonnet off,
  And placed her mother's chair.

And then beside the pot she set
  The caddy full of tea,
And laid the neck-tie in a place,
  Where George was sure to see.

The happiness and joy there was,
  I really could not tell;
But families who dwell in love,
  They know it very well.

And sure our blessed Saviour feels
  Joy in his home above,
When here upon this earth he sees
  A dwelling full of love.

THE GLEANERS.

Some busy weeks had passed away,
  With all the summer heat;
And autumn came and harvest time,
  With sheaves of golden wheat.

And blackberries were in the hedge,
  And nuts were in the wood,
And children with their baskets went
  To get them where they could.

And apples hung with rosy cheeks,
  In all the gardens round,
And laughing boys climbed up the trees,
  To shake them to the ground.

The village school was broken up,
  That all might lend a hand
To gather in the ripened corn,
  That gladdened all the land.

And oh! it was a pleasant sight,
  To see the gleaners come,
At evening with their sheaves of corn,
  Rejoicing to their home.

And oh! it was a pleasant sight,
  O'er all the sunny plain,
To see the children picking up
  The scattered ears of grain.

Then sitting underneath a tree,
To eat their meal at noon;
Then singing home at eventide,
Beneath the harvest moon.

Both Mary Day and Lucy Bell,
And little Nelly White,
Were mostly gleaning in the fields,
From early morn till night.

For Mary said that she must work,
And never think of play,
That they might have some corn to grind,
Against the winter's day.

And wheresoever Mary gleaned,
There Lucy you might see,
At work beside her in the field,
And talking earnestly.

The other girls seemed much surprised;
They all were at a loss,
What could be come to Lucy Bell!
She was not half so cross.

"I don't think so," said Susan Brand,
"She's very cross, I say;
She hardly ever speaks to me,
And goes with Mary Day."

"Well, all the girls like Mary Day,
Of course," said Jenny Lee,
"I think she is as nice a girl,
As you would ever see."

"Oh yes; she's very nice, no doubt,"
Retorted Susan Brand,
"I call her a deceitful snake,
To steal away my friend."

The girls disliked sharp Susan Brand,
They knew her temper well;
And that she'd always been the friend
Of peevish Lucy Bell.

And did not for a moment think
That Mary was to blame;
And when they heard her called a snake,
They said it was a shame.

But Nelly White burst into tears,
Her face was in a glow;
"Oh! Mary Day is not a snake,
No one shall call her so!"

Then all the girls laughed heartily,
And said that she was right,
"That Mary Day was not a snake,"
Nor little Nelly White."

Then Susan Brand walked further off,
And cried, "I do not care!"
Oh, little boys and little girls!
Of these bad words beware.

For those who do not care to-day,
Will have to care to-morrow;
It is the nearest way that leads
To sin, and shame, and sorrow.

THE EARNEST TALK.

Lucy. And do you quite believe that God
Hears every word I say?
I always think that heaven seems
So very far away.

When I look in the sky at night,
And all is still and clear,
And fancy God above the stars,
I think He cannot hear.

Mary. The Bible says He's everywhere,
Although we cannot see;
Yes, even in this harvest field,
Observing you and me.

Lucy. But you don't think so, I suppose,
It never can be true,
That God would listen to the words,
That now I say to you.

I should be quite afraid to speak,
If this could really be;
But 'tis not likely He would watch
Young girls like you and me.

Mary. The Bible says that every thought,
As well as every word,
Of every person in the world,
Is known unto the Lord.

Lucy. That's very dreadful! don't you think,
  If we were in a mine,
Down in the earth, far out of sight,
  Where sun could never shine,

That we could well be hidden there?
  Because in such a hole,
No one could possibly look down,
  To see into your soul.

Mary. The Bible says in heaven or hell,
  Or on the furthest sea,
Where darkness covers every thing,
  Still He will present be.

He sees us when we rise at morn,
  And in our beds at night,
And whether we're at work or play,
  We're always in His sight.

Lucy. I hope He does not watch *me* so,
  It makes me quite afraid,
I should not like to think that God
  Was close beside my bed.

My mother says when I do wrong,
  Or e'en a falsehood tell,
He will be sure to punish me,
  And shut me up in hell.

And that He keeps a dreadful book,
  That He will judge me by,
Where all my sins are written down,
  With every little lie.

Mary. My mother does not speak like that,
It is her great delight,
To know that God will condescend
To keep us in His sight.

He does not watch to punish us,
Or shut us out of heaven;
Because you know He gave his Son,
That we might be forgiven.

And don't you think that Jesus Christ,
Was very full of love,
When for our sakes He came to earth,
And left His home above;

And lived for more than thirty years,
Like any poor man's child?
A humble life of poverty,
And like a poor man toiled.

When *I* think of the love He shewed,
It makes me fit to cry,
To know that He should lose His life,
For such an one as I.

I often tell Him how I long
To please Him if I could;
And how I'll try to copy Him,
By being kind and good.

And how I hope that I shall grow
More patient every day,
And learn to think of others first,
Nor wish to get my way.

Oh! if we could but grow like Christ,
  How happy we should be,
And I should like to live for Him,
  Who is so kind to me.

I am so sorry, when I've been
  Unkind to any one;
Or been put out, or done a thing
  That I should not have done.

Lucy. I want to ask you something more,
  But now 'tis getting late;
My mother said I should be home,
  Before the sun was set.

Mary. Then let us set off instantly,
  But only do behold
The sunshine coming through the trees,
  Like glittering rays of gold.

I always like to see the sun
  Sink down into the west,
He drops so still and peacefully,
  As if he went to rest.

And all the clouds are in a glow,
  Of purple, gold, and green,
And sometimes there's a bit of sky,
  Of clear blue sky between.

With little golden clouds at rest,
  So beautifully bright;
I often think that heaven's gate,
  Must there be just in sight."

And thus they chatted on their way,
Of things that Mary knew,
Nor heeded that their footprints lay
Upon the evening dew.

THE MOONLIGHT WALK.

And now the harvest time is past,
And all the golden corn
Had been cut down and stored away
In stacks, or in the barn.

The gleaner left the stubble field,
And with her latest store,
Walked wearily and thankfully
To her own cottage door.

The full round moon looked calmly down,
'Twas almost light as day,
Except where shadows of the trees
Across the footpath lay.

And Mary Day and Lucy Bell,
Paced on with quiet feet,
As loth to break the silent calm,
That fell so pure and sweet.

The beetle's wing cut through the air,
  And made a ringing sound,
And bats went flitting to and fro,
  And circling round and round.

But still the girls walked side by side,
  And neither cared to speak,
Till Mary saw a twinkling tear
  Slide down poor Lucy's cheek.

Mary. "What was it, dear, the other night,
  You said you wished to ask?"
But Lucy answered with a sigh,
  To speak, was now a task.

Again she sighed, and then she spoke,
  Her words were very low—
Lucy. "Can you forgive me, what I did?
  That wicked thing, you know."

Mary. "Oh yes! I have, indeed, I have,
  Pray do not cry and grieve;
I'll never think of it again,
  I won't, you may believe.

"I did forgive you from the first."
Lucy. "Oh! that was good of you,
I thought that you would hate me so,
  Directly that you knew."

Mary. "Oh! don't say so, I could not hate
  A person if I tried;
And then you looked so very sad,
  And were so vexed beside.

"I would have told you so before,
But I knew very well,
That you were never fond of me,
Now were you, Lucy Bell?"

Lucy. "No, Mary! I was so provoked,
Because you were so good,
And many a spiteful thing I've done,
To harm you if I could.

"But when the rain came down that night,
And you took so much care
To shelter me, and not yourself,
Well, that I could not bear!

"And then I thought that I would try
At once to copy you;
And every day I've loved you more,
And now, indeed, I do.

"But oh! 'tis hard to be like you,
I'm always doing wrong;
My temper is so bad, you know,
And then, my will is strong."

Mary. "Then don't you ever pray to God,
To take your will away!"

Lucy. "No! that I've never done at all,
I don't know how to pray.

"But will you teach me, if you know?
I really wish to try;
But God perhaps won't notice me,
I've often told a lie."

Mary. "Oh yes! He will, for Jesus' sake,
Who shed His precious blood,
On purpose to wash out our sins,
And make us true and good.

"And if you ask Him earnestly,
And mean the thing you say,
I'm very sure that you will find,
He'll hear you when you pray.

"Because God is our Father, dear,
And not our enemy,
And 'tis His will and pleasure too
To fit us for the sky.

"So when you find your will is strong,
Or temper hard to break,
Say, 'Help me, by thy Spirit, Lord,
For Christ my Saviour's sake.'

"I've often found, when things were hard,
And I could not get through,
That when I prayed, I did them soon,
And found them pleasant too.

"You need not be at all afraid,
Don't think it is a task;
For God is far more quick to help,
Than we are free to ask."

LUCY'S PRAYER.

Perhaps you think that Lucy Bell
Was now quite satisfied;
As Mary had forgiven her,
And no one knew beside.

But she was not—she truly said,
"Her money I have had,
And I shall not be satisfied,
Until it is repaid.

"My mother has some shirts to make
For Dr. James, I know."
Now Mistress Bell had been well taught,
When she was young to sew;

And being very sharply pressed
To settle Charmin's bill,
She took the Doctor's shirts to make,
And worked with right good will.

And Lucy, though she hated work,
Could use her needle well,
And when she chose, few girls could sew
So quick as Lucy Bell.

"Mother," she said, "you won't object
To let me make a shirt;
I'll promise you to do it well,
And keep it free from dirt."

Her mother quickly raised her head,
  She was not sure she heard;
"You make a shirt, and keep it clean!
  Child, don't be so absurd!"

"Mother, I mean what I have said,
  You know I can work well;
'Tis money that I want to earn:"
  "For what?" said Mistress Bell.

"Some foolish nonsense, I suppose,
  "But you may have your way;
And this industrious fit, I guess,
  Will last you just a day.

"However, if you make the shirt,
  The money I'll advance;"
And Mistress Bell laughed heartily,
  To think how small the chance.

But Lucy made her no reply,
  She knew 't would be a trial,
The hardest lesson she had had
  In real self-denial.

And thus she reasoned with herself,
  "I know that Mary Day,
If she had such a thing to do,
  Would think 'twas best to pray.

"She said when things were difficult,
  And what she could not bear,
She managed them quite easily,
  If first she went to prayer.

"I'll do the same;" and Lucy sank
  Down gently on her knee:
"Help me, O Lord! to work, that I
  An honest girl may be."

"And give me patience to get through
  This work I undertake;
And bless me with thy Spirit, Lord,
  For Christ my Saviour's sake."

Then Lucy rose up from her knees,
  A tear was in her eye;
And yet she felt much happier;
  We know the reason why.

For God had heard that secret prayer,
  And answered it in love,
And quick as lightning came to her,
  His Spirit from above.

And Lucy then sat down to sew,
  Her heart felt very light;
"My work is pleasant now," she said,
  "And Mary Day was right."

When little Patty came and pulled
  The cotton off her lap,
She took it gently from her hand,
  Without a word or slap.

'Twas not at all an easy task
  That Lucy had to do;
And had she not both worked and prayed,
  She would not have got through.

She had to go to school each day,
And make the shirt, you know;
So all her play-time she gave up,
That she might sit and sew.

Her mother was surprised indeed,
And thought it would not last;
Still wondered what could make the child
Work on so very fast.

She fancied Lucy's temper too,
Was not so rough and cross;
But what had made the difference,
She still was at a loss.

And still the work went briskly on,
For still did Lucy ask
For patience, and a right good will,
To help her through the task.

When she had prayed she went to work,
She did not loiter then;
And if she found her temper rise,
She prayed, and tried again.

And every time that Lucy prayed,
God heard her earnest prayer,
And His good Spirit came to help,
The patient worker there.

NELLY'S SECRET.

"I've got a little secret now,
That you will like to hear;"
And Nelly put her rosy mouth
Close up to Mary's ear.

"As I was running home from school,
I tripped my foot and fell,
And then I cried, and close behind
Was coming Lucy Bell.

"She ran at once and helped me up,
And said, 'Nell, are you hurt?
Come, let me wipe your frock and hands,
They're covered with the dirt.'

"So then she rubbed them nice and clean,
And spoke so very kind;
'But look,' she said, 'you've torn a slit
Down in your frock behind.

"'But I have got my needle here,
I'll mend it in a trice;'
And then she ran it quickly up—
Do look! so neat and nice.

"And when I thanked her, then she said,
'My thanks I owe to you;
Don't you remember lending me,
Your pencil long ago?

"'I was so very cross and rude,
I did not thank you then;
Forgive me, Nelly, and I wont
Reward you so again.'"

"Well, dear, and then, what did you say,
When she talked of reward?"
"I put my arms about her neck,
And hugged her very hard.

"And then she said, 'I've often been
Unkind to you before;'
Don't mind, I said, you will not be
Ill-natured any more."

"And she said, 'No; I mean to be
Like your friend, Mary Day;'
And then she kissed my face again,
And so she went away.

"You said she would be good at last,
If I would only wait;
And she was very good to day,
And has been so of late."

"Yes, I do really think she means
To gain a better name;
And all the girls observe the change,
And say she's not the same.

"And she was gathering blackberries
Along the hedge one day,
To take them home for little Pat;
That was not Lucy's way.

"This week she's sitting very close
At needle-work, I know;
I can't think why she's doing that,
She never liked to sew."

"Oh! let's be kind to every one,"
Said little Nelly White;
And her sweet happy childish face,
Glowed crimson with delight.

LUCY AN HONEST GIRL.

Now autumn days were growing short,
With heavy dews at night;
And often in the early morn,
The grass was frosty white.

And woodland paths were damp and still,
Save when the rustling breeze
Shook down the yellow, withered leaves,
In showers from the trees.

And all the little birds that sung
So gaily in the spring,
Were gone away to foreign parts,
Or did not choose to sing;

Except the robin, who abides
With us the seasons round,
And comes still closer to our door,
When snow is on the ground.

Then he will sing and sing again,
His sweet and mellow lay,
Till evening shades steal o'er the sky,
And daylight fades away.

I often think that God has tuned
That little robin's voice,
To bid us keep a thankful heart,
And evermore rejoice.

And often Lucy heard him sing,
When it was nearly dark,
As with a patient industry
She laboured at her work.

At last the Doctor's shirt was done,
In every part complete,
And even Mistress Bell confessed
The work was very neat.

"Well, mother, after all, I think,
I rather like to sew."
"Yes, child, you've worked with right good will,
And have the habit now;

"And that makes all the difference
Of liking it or no,
Which you will find in many things,
As through the world you go."

And now her mother paid her well,
She fully kept her word,
And Lucy with her money, was
As happy as a bird.

"I now shall be an honest girl,
At least I'll pay my debt,
And this hard lesson I have learned,
I never shall forget."

At school next day, the work-bag lay,
As it before had done,
And Lucy popped the shilling in,
Observed by only one.

But Lucy saw dear Mary's look
Of pleased and glad surprise,
And quickly said, "Don't say a word,"
While tears filled both their eyes.

Not tears of grief, but tears of joy,
They loved each other more,
Now each had done her duty well,
Than ere they did before.

THE DAY OF REST.

It was the day of rest—a pleasant day,
The quiet sunshine in the churchyard lay,
Where the old stones, with moss and ivy
crowned,
Watched o'er the loved ones, sleeping in the
ground.
The bells ceased ringing, and you then might
hear
The organ's peal rise solemnly and clear,
And then the low confession and the prayer,
That God, our Father, would be present there.
The children of the Sunday School took part,
Chanting the anthems, they had learned by heart;
'Twas sweet to hear their youthful voices raise,
The grand Te Deum and the psalm of praise;
And see them lowly on the bended knee,
Making responses to the Litany:
And then to hear the general "Amen,"
Where children's voices intermixed again.
The Pastor was a minister who gave
His anxious care that little flock to save;
It was their hearts' consent he wished to gain,
And therefore always made his sermons plain,
That even children when they went away,
Could many portions of the sermon say:

And many thought they certainly would try
To gain that home eternal in the sky,
Which he described so beautiful and blest,
So full of happiness and peaceful rest;—
And other hearers as they left the place,
Resolved to seek their Heavenly Father's face.
This day the minister addressed the young,
And kind persuasive words flowed from his tongue;
He counselled them to seek the Lord betimes,
Ere strong temptation led to deeper crimes;
He told of God's free love, and how he sent
His own dear Son, to bear sin's punishment,
And begged that all, who then his counsel heard,—
Would give their hearts in earnest to the Lord.

When all was over, and the people gone,
Mary and Lucy sauntered home alone.
No need to hasten, and it soon was clear
Lucy had thoughts for Mary's willing ear;
"Mary," she said, "I'm trying to be good,
I really wish to give my heart to God.
What does that mean? How can I give my heart,
Take up the cross, and choose the better part?
And what's the meaning of the Christian's walk?
Is it the things they *do*, as well as talk?
What should they do? and what's the difference
Between the good, and those who make pretence?"

Mary.

Good people love the Lord who died for men,
And think they cannot do enough again;

They always wish His precepts to obey,
And copy His example every day.

Lucy.
Well, do describe it very clear and plain,
And if I'm stupid, tell it me again.

Mary.
I'll do the best I'm able, Lucy Bell,
My mother knows it, and explains it well.
She teaches me, when we are at our work,
I only wish that you could hear *her* talk;
Religion seems so pleasant and so good,
You would not do without it, if you could.

Lucy.
That's how I feel when I'm along with you,
Which makes me wish to know just what you do,
And what religion is.

Mary.
Well, let me see,
It's very plain as mother talks to me;
It all is love, and being good and kind,
And meek and patient with a humble mind:
Not discontented, though we may be poor,
And glad that other people should have more.
And never to be proud of what we know,
Or scorning others, who are dull and slow;—
But to assist them, and without pretence,
And never looking for a recompense.

And mother says, we always should be glad
When folks do right, and sorry if they are bad:
Nor should we talk about their evil ways,
But still be always pleased if we can praise;
She says we should go on, and persevere,
And keep a cheerful face, and never fear;
And if things do not happen as we would,
To bear it patiently, and trust in God;
Because He's able, if 'tis best to cure,
If not, He'll give us power to endure.
And mother says, it never is a loss,
To follow Jesus and take up our cross;
For if we do His will, then we shall know
His blessed truth, and like our Saviour grow.

Lucy.

Do you do all these things? said Lucy Bell.

Mary.

I wish to do, but cannot do them well.
I wish I could, but still I mean to try,
And hope at last to gain the victory;
Because you know we are not left alone,
We have the Spirit of the Blessed One;
He speaks within our hearts as with a tongue,
And says, "Now this is right, and that is wrong."

Lucy.

Oh yes! I know it—I have felt just so,
Since I determined I would better grow.

Is that the Spirit? It is very near,
It seems as if it spoke within your ear;
Then I suppose we should not disobey?

Mary.

No! never, Lucy, lest He go away;
And we be left without a friend to guide,
And Satan watching us, to make us slide.

Lucy.

But if we do go wrong, and errors make,
Will God forgive us then for Jesus' sake?

Mary.

Yes, if we are sorry, and confess our sin,
And still are earnest and sincere within.

Lucy.

I hope I shall be earnest, Mary Day;
I am so glad you taught me how to pray,
For when I've prayed, I really feel as though
I'd gained a better mind and will, you know.

Mary.

Ah, yes!—that's how I feel, so well content;
But Lucy, dear, do read the Testament:
It shews so plainly how we are forgiven,
And how God wishes we should go to heaven,
To live for ever in that glorious place,
And see our blessed Saviour face to face.

Lucy.

But there's one thing you have not mentioned yet,
And that is what I never shall forget;
No—I shall always recollect the hour,
When you o'ertook me in that stormy shower,
And were so kind and helped me all you could,
And thus returned my evil, all with good;
That broke my heart at last, and made me see
The mighty difference between you and me.

Mary.

Oh! I did little, Mary quick replied;
Our Lord did *that* when He was crucified:
He said, as then his latest breath He drew,
"Father, forgive; they know not what they do."

And thus the dear companions gently walk,
Their young hearts burning, as of Him they talk;
He joined Himself unto them by the way,
And blessed the children on that Sabbath-day.

CHRISTMAS EVE.

'Twas winter time and Christmas Eve,
Long looked for now had come,
And separated families
Were gathering at home.

Where loving hearts and busy hands,
Made neither stop nor stay,
To have a real Christmas feast
On happy Christmas-day.

The boys had been into the woods,
Or down the sandy lane,
For branches from the holly trees
To deck the window-pane.

The sun had set with crimson clouds,
It was a frosty night,
And every little star looked down
With penetrating light.

And all the trees stood stiff and cold,
Their barren branches crossed,
Whilst sparkling lay on every spray,
A feathery fringe of frost.

So bright it was, so clear and still,
That as you listening stood,
You plainly heard the horses feet—
Upon the turnpike road.

From early morn till afternoon
Did George and Mary work,
And swiftly passed the busy hours,
With jokes and merry talk.

George had been down to Charmin's shop,
With cash in hand to pay,
For nuts and other dainty things,
To eat on Christmas day.

How cheerful did the dwelling look!
First coming in from night;
With all the shining holly twigs
And scarlet berries bright.

And now it is by George proposed,
To which they all agree;
To laugh and chat a little bit,
Before they get their tea.

So round about the glowing fire,
They quickly take their place;
And warmly fell the ruddy light,
On every happy face.

"Do, Mary, look at Mother now,"
Said George with glad surprise,
"She looks so rosy and so well,
I can't take off my eyes."

"And mother says she *is* quite well,"
And Mary kissed her cheek;
"Now are you sure your leg is strong?
And don't you feel it weak?"

"'Tis really strong, my darling girl,
So put away your fears,
I have not felt myself so well,
For nearly twenty years."

"Hurrah!" said George—"now little Poll,
We'll keep her strong—we will;
She shan't be slaving at the work,
Whilst we are sitting still."

"No; no, indeed; were father here,
We should have Christmas fun;"
"He may come yet—trust me," said George,
He'll do what can be done."

"I know my mother thinks he'll come,
But won't say so for fear;
Now, mother, tell the honest truth,
You think he will be here?"

"I thought we should have had him home,
Before the year was out;
When last he wrote from Trinidad,
There seemed but little doubt."

"He's sure to come; the 'Orient,'
He says, is tight and tough;
I think I'll go to sea, mother,
When I am old enough."

"There, George, don't talk about that now,"—
Beside, I hear the gate,
And footsteps coming up the path,
'Tis some one calling late."

George sprung at once to ope the door,
"There now, I told you so;
Here's father all alive and well,
Himself from top to toe."

They fly to bring the good man in,
With cries of glad surprise;
And Mary and her mother say,
They can't believe their eyes.

They take his hat, his rough sea coat,
They pull him to the fire;
And every one has twenty things,
That moment to enquire.

"Well, let me get my breath," said he,
"I'm dazzled with the light;
And let me see your faces first,
For that's the finest sight.

My dear! he said, and kissed his wife,
You're looking charmingly;
Full ten years younger, I should say,
Than when I went to sea."

At this George gave a knowing wink,
And Mary caught his eye;
"He'll hear of all from mother soon,
She'll tell him by and bye."

"And how's my little Polly here?"
The happy father said,
And kissed his daughter's glowing cheek,
And fondly stroked her head.

Upon my word, a bonny lass
Our little maid will be;
And here's my boy run up so tall,
He'll soon be fit for sea.

"I think they've kept my charge right well,
To care for you, my dear;
They have not broke their mother's heart,
I see that very clear."

The happy wife then spoke, and told
  The tale we know so well;
And oh! it was a pleasant tale
  To hear, as well as tell.

"God bless them both," the father said;
  A tear stood in his eye;
"With such a wife and children too,
  A happy man am I.

"God bless you both," he said again,
  "God bless us all, I pray,
And let us bless His Providence
  That here we meet to day."

A moment's pause of grateful joy,
  Then round the board they met;
If there be greater happiness,
  I have not seen it yet.

JARROLD AND SONS, PRINTERS, NORWICH.

CPSIA information can be obtained
at www.ICGtesting.com
Printed in the USA
LVHW111509230223
740229LV00002B/75

9 783382 306670